THE MERRY ADVENTURES OF ROBIN HOOD

Library of Congress Cataloging-in-Publication Data

Mattern, Joanne, (date)
    The merry adventures of Robin Hood / by Howard Pyle; retold by
Joanne Mattern; illustrated by Susi Kilgore.
       p.   cm. (Troll illustrated classics)
    Summary: Recounts the legend of Robin Hood, who plundered the
king's purse and poached his deer and whose generosity endeared him
to the poor.
    ISBN 0-8167-2858-5 (lib. bdg.)   ISBN 0-8167-2859-3 (pbk.)
    1. Robin Hood (Legendary character)—Legends. [1. Robin Hood
(Legendary character) 2. Folklore—England.] I. Kilgore, Susi, ill.
II. Pyle, Howard, 1853-1911. Merry adventures of Robin Hood.
III. Title.
PZ81.M427Me 1993
398.22—dc20   92-12702

Printed in the United States of America.
10 9 8 7 6 5 4 3 2 1

THE MERRY ADVENTURES OF ROBIN HOOD

HOWARD PYLE

Retold by
Joanne Mattern

Illustrated by
Susi Kilgore

Troll Associates

In merry England in days of old, there lived within Sherwood Forest, near Nottingham Town, a famous outlaw whose name was Robin Hood. No archer ever lived who had such skill and cunning, nor were there ever such men as those who roamed with him through the greenwood. They all lived happily, wanting nothing.

Even though Robin and all of his men were outlaws, they were much loved by the country folk, for no one ever came to Robin for help and went away empty-handed.

And now here is the story of how Robin became an outlaw and came to dwell in Sherwood Forest.

When Robin was a youth of eighteen, the Sheriff of Nottingham proclaimed a shooting match and offered a prize to the best archer in Nottinghamshire. Robin took his stout yew bow and a score of arrows, and started off from Locksley Town through Sherwood Forest to Nottingham.

As he walked through the bright spring day with a brisk step and a merry whistle, he came upon some foresters seated beneath a great oak tree, making themselves merry with feasting. One of them called out to Robin, ''Where do you go, little lad, with your one-penny bow and your farthing shafts?''

Robin grew angry at their teasing. "My bow and my arrows are as good as yours," he said. "I am going to the shooting match at Nottingham, and I will win the prize."

At this, the foresters laughed and teased some more, and Robin grew even angrier. "Look, at the glade's end is a herd of deer," he said boldly. "I'll bet you twenty marks that I can strike the best of them with my arrow."

"Done!" cried one of the foresters.

Robin took his yew bow in his hand and placed an arrow to the bowstring. The next moment, the arrow sped down the glade. The noblest deer of all the herd leaped up, then fell dead with Robin's arrow in him.

"How do you like that shot, good fellow?" asked Robin, laughing. "I have won the bet!"

Then all the foresters were filled with rage. "You'll have no money from me," said the one who had made the bet. "Get away from here before I beat you!"

"You have shot the King's deer," said another. "That is against the law!"

Robin looked at the foresters with a grim face, then turned and walked away. But the forester was angry that Robin had won the bet. Without any warning, he grabbed his bow and sent an arrow flying after Robin.

Luckily, the arrow missed, whistling by not three inches from Robin's head. Robin turned and sent an arrow back in return. The shaft flew straight and true, and the forester fell forward with a cry, the arrow wet with his heart's blood. Then, before the others could follow, Robin dashed off into the greenwood. All the joy was gone from the day, for he had killed a man.

And so Robin came to dwell in the forest. He was an outlaw, not only because he had killed a man, but because he had also poached the King's deer. Two hundred pounds were set upon his head as a reward for anyone who brought him to the King.

The Sheriff of Nottingham was determined to bring Robin to justice. Not only did he want the two hundred pounds, but the forester Robin had killed was his kin. And so the Sheriff became Robin's sworn enemy.

In time, Robin Hood gathered a band of many other folk who came to Sherwood to escape wrongdoing or oppression. They made Robin Hood their leader, and swore that they would take what the rich and powerful had unjustly gained, and give these gains to the poor instead.

One morning when all the birds were singing, Robin Hood went to the edges of Sherwood to seek adventure. He watched the road while many different people went by, but found nothing of excitement.

Finally, he walked along a road that dipped toward a broad stream. A narrow log bridge spanned the rushing water. As Robin started across, he spotted a stranger,

nearly seven feet tall, stepping onto the bridge from the other side.

"Stand back," Robin called, "and let the better man cross first."

"I am the better man, and it is you who should stand back," replied the stranger.

"We shall see. Let us fight to see which of us is the stronger."

"You are a coward," the stranger shot back. "You have a bow to shoot at my heart, while I have nothing but a plain staff."

"Never have I had a coward's name!" Robin cried. "I will lay down my bow and arrows, and cut a staff of my own to fight you."

The tall stranger agreed, and waited on the bridge while Robin cut a staff of oak, six feet in length. Then Robin leaped back onto the bridge and headed for the giant.

Never did the Knights of Arthur's Round Table meet in a stouter fight. Each man struck mighty blows, until they were all bumped and bruised. But neither one cried, "Enough!" or fell into the water, so evenly were they matched.

Finally, Robin struck such a blow to the taller man's ribs, it seemed he would fall into the water. But the giant kept his balance and thwacked Robin so hard, the outlaw fell head over heels into the stream. "And where are you now?" cried the stranger, roaring with laughter.

"Oh, floating away with the tide," Robin called back, spluttering. Then he, too, began to laugh at his plight as he splashed his way to the bank.

The stranger helped Robin to dry land. Then Robin blew a note on his horn, and soon all the merry band had joined them beside the stream.

"Good master," said Will Stutely, "why are you wet from head to foot?"

"This stout fellow has tumbled me into the water, and given me a fair beating besides."

"Then he shall not go without a dunking and a beating himself!" cried Will, as all the men started forward.

"No, stop," Robin commanded, "for he is a good man, and no harm shall befall him. Good youth," he said to the giant, "will you join our band and be my right-hand man? Will you be one of my merry men?"

"Yes, I will," the tall man agreed.

"What is your name?"

"Men call me John Little," he replied.

Then Will Stutely, who loved a good jest, spoke up. "That will not do. Because you are so small and thin, we will call you Little John!"

Then Robin Hood and all his men laughed and agreed that this was the perfect name for the giant. And so Little John joined the band and became Robin's right-hand man.

The Sheriff of Nottingham thought of little else besides capturing Robin Hood, for it angered him that he and his men flaunted the laws so boldly. "If I could only persuade Robin Hood to come to Nottingham, I would lay hands upon him so hard that he would never get away," the Sheriff said. Then it came to him that the best way to catch Robin Hood would be to proclaim a great shooting match. Surely Robin Hood could not pass up a chance to show off his archery skills—and then the Sheriff would have him!

And so he sent messengers north, south, east, and west, to proclaim news of the great match everywhere. Everyone was bidden to come, and the prize would be an arrow of pure gold.

When Robin heard the news, he gathered all the men of his band and said, "I would like one of us to win the golden arrow, both because it is a fair prize and because our friend the Sheriff is offering it. Let us all go to the match."

Then David of Doncaster said, "But master, I have heard that this is nothing but a trap the Sheriff has laid to catch you. I beg you, do not go!"

"Shall we have it said that Robin Hood was afraid of the Sheriff of Nottingham? No, David, what you have told me makes me want the prize more than ever. We will go to the match in disguise, and one of us will win the golden arrow."

Nottingham Town was a fair sight on the day of the shooting match. All the people who lived thereabouts had come to see the great event. They sat in rows of benches along the field. A large tent had been set up on the grass, and here gathered all the archers who were to compete. Never had such a company of men gathered as was at Nottingham that day, for the very best archers of merry England had come to try their skill and win the prize.

At last, the Sheriff and his lady arrived on their horses, and went to take their seats at the head of the field. Then the herald announced the rules, and the contest began.

As each man took his turn, the Sheriff studied him carefully, anxious to see if Robin Hood was among the crowd. But he saw no one clad in the Lincoln green that was worn by Robin and his men. "Never mind," the Sheriff said to himself. "Surely he is here, and I just cannot find him in this great crowd."

The afternoon drew on, with each archer taking his turn at the target. Finally, only three men were left—the three best archers of the day. Two, Gill o' the Red Cap and Adam o' the Dell, were well known to the crowd. But the third was a stranger with tattered clothing and a patch over one eye, whom no one recognized.

Each man took his turn. Adam o' the Dell's shaft struck the center of the target, but was close to the outside of the ring. Then Gill o' the Red Cap shot, and his arrow lodged almost at the very center.

"Well done, Gilbert!" the Sheriff shouted joyfully. "I think that the prize is yours. Let me see you shoot better than that," he challenged the ragged stranger.

The stranger spoke not a word, but stood very still as he took his aim. The arrow flew straight, and so true that it struck a feather off Gill's shaft as it passed. Then the arrow lodged in the very center of the target. No one in the crowd said anything. They could only look at each other in amazement.

The Sheriff came down to where the stranger stood, leaning upon his bow while all the people crowded close to see who it was that shot so wondrously well. "Here, good fellow," said the Sheriff, handing him the golden arrow. "Take the prize, for you have won it fairly. What is your name, and where do you come from?"

"Men call me Jock o' Teviotdale," said the stranger.

"Well, Jock, you are the fairest archer I have ever seen. If you will join my service, I will clothe you better than what you wear now, and your food and drink shall be the very best. I trust you draw a better bow than that coward, Robin Hood, who dared not show his face today. Tell me, good fellow, will you join my service?"

"No, I will not," the stranger replied. "I will be my own man, and no one will be my master."

"Then get away from here," the Sheriff shouted, his voice trembling with anger, "before I have you beaten for your insolence!" Turning on his heel, the Sheriff strode away.

In Sherwood's depths later that day, a very odd company gathered. Some were dressed as beggars, others as tinkers, and still more as friars. In the middle sat one dressed in tattered scarlet, with a patch over one eye. In one hand he clutched a golden arrow. There was much laughing and shouting as the man stripped off his ragged clothes to reveal a suit of Lincoln green. For it was Robin Hood himself who had won the prize from the Sheriff's hand.

Then all sat down to a woodland feast and talked of the joke they had played upon the Sheriff. But Robin drew Little John aside and said, ''Today I heard the Sheriff say, 'You shoot better than that coward, Robin Hood.' I want to let him know who it was that won the prize, for I am no coward.''

Little John said, ''Good master, take me and Will Stutely, and we will send the Sheriff news of all this by a messenger he will not expect.''

So it was that, as the Sheriff sat down to eat in the great hall of his house at Nottingham, something fell among the dishes on the table. One of the men-at-arms picked it up and brought it to the Sheriff. Everyone saw it was a gray goose shaft with a fine scroll tied near its head. The Sheriff opened the scroll, and his cheeks grew red with rage. This is what the message said:

> *Now Heaven bless thy grace this day,*
> *Say all in sweet Sherwood,*
> *For thou didst give the prize away*
> *To merry Robin Hood.*

''Where did this come from?'' the Sheriff asked in a mighty voice.

''Through the window, your worship,'' said the man-at-arms. And so the Sheriff found out who had won the golden arrow from his very own hand that day.

One bright, sunny day in May, Will Stutely and Will Scarlet and some other members of the merry band were out walking through Sherwood. After they had gone some distance, Will Stutely suddenly stopped. "Wait!" he said. "I think I hear the sound of someone in distress."

All listened closely. Sure enough, the sound of a person weeping came from the side of the path.

"Let us see what the trouble is," said Will Scarlet, and the men headed into the trees to see what they could find.

Soon they came across a pond. At the side of the water lay a young man, weeping loudly. On a branch above his head hung a beautiful harp of polished wood inlaid with gold.

"Who are you, fellow, lying there killing all the grass with salt water?" called Will Stutely. At that, the young man jumped up and faced them.

"I know this lad," said another of the band. "He is a minstrel whom I have seen in these parts many times. But never have I seen him so downcast!"

Will Scarlet laid his hand on the young man's shoulder. "Come with us, lad. We know someone who may be able to aid you in your distress."

The youth did as he was asked, and the band made its way back through the forest to the glade where Robin and his men lived. They walked through the camp until they came to the greenwood tree and found Robin Hood and Little John sitting beneath it.

The youth recognized Robin, and he grew afraid. But Robin told him, "Cheer up, lad, for we will help you out of your difficulties. What is your name?"

"Allan a Dale," the young minstrel replied.

"Tell us your troubles, and we will see what we can do to help."

So the youth told his tale. He had traveled all through England, singing and playing. Sometimes he stayed in small villages, other times at castles or farms. It was at one of these farms that he met sweet Ellen o' the Dale and fell in love with her. Ellen loved him, too, and so they vowed to be true to one another forever.

But Ellen's father had discovered what was happening, and he took Ellen away and arranged for her to marry Sir Stephen of Trent in two days' time. Ellen wanted nothing to do with that marriage, but her father would not listen to her pleas. "Ellen is soft and gentle," Allan finished. "She will do her father's bidding, but her heart will break and she will die."

"I think I have a plan that might help you, Allan," said Robin Hood. "You and not Sir Stephen will wed fair Ellen on her wedding morn. But to do this requires a priest. I cannot think of any who will help us."

Will Scarlet spoke up, saying, "I know of a friar who might help you. He dwells at a spot in the woods called Fountain Abbey. I know the place well, and can lead you there."

"Then give me your hand, Allan!" cried Robin. "I swear to you that by this time two days hence, Ellen o' the Dale shall be your wife. We will go visit this friar of Fountain Abbey tomorrow to arrange matters."

One of the band came to say that dinner was ready, and so Robin led the others to where a tasty feast was spread on the grass. The meal was a merry one. Even Allan laughed with the rest, for his cheeks were flushed with the hope that Robin Hood had given him.

The friar of Fountain Abbey, who preferred to go by the name Friar Tuck, was soon located. He was a jolly sort, fond of a good jest, and quickly agreed to Robin's plans to bring Allan and Ellen together.

The men of Sherwood Forest rose early on the day that Ellen o' the Dale was to be married. After they had finished breakfast, Robin chose a score of good men to go with him. He dressed in the colorful clothes of a strolling minstrel, and slung a harp across his shoulder. Then the merry band set out for the little church where fair Ellen was to be married.

All was quiet at the church. The men hid themselves in the long grass and bushes, and rested for a bit. Soon young David of Doncaster spied an old friar coming up to the door, rattling his keys.

"Go down and talk to your brother of the cloth," Robin said to Friar Tuck. "Then get yourself into the church, so you will be there when we need you."

So Friar Tuck went down and made the acquaintance of the old priest. Upon hearing that Tuck wanted no more than to rest in the cool shade of the church and observe the wedding, the other priest gladly let him in.

Robin sent Little John and Will Stutely into the church, while he went to sit on a bench outside the door. Presently, six churchmen came riding down the road. Among them were the Bishop of Hereford and the Prior of Emmet.

When the holy men came up to the door of the church, they caught sight of Robin dressed in his colorful clothes. "Hello, good fellow," said the Bishop. "Who are you that comes here in such bright feathers?"

"A harper am I from the North country," said Robin, "and I can play better than any other man in all of England. If I may play at the wedding, I promise that I will cause the fair bride to love the man she marries as long as they live together."

"Is it so?" asked the Bishop, staring at Robin in amazement. "This maiden has bewitched my cousin Stephen. If you can cause her to love the man she is to marry, I will give you whatever you ask. Let me have a taste of your skill, fellow."

"No," Robin replied. "I will not play until the bride and groom come."

Just then, a group riding on horses came around the bend of the road. First was Sir Stephen. Beside him rode Edward of Deirwold, Ellen's father. Then came a litter drawn by two horses, and inside it was the fair Ellen. At the end of the line rode six men-at-arms, the sunlight flashing on their steel caps as they jingled down the dusty road.

When they came to the door of the church, Sir Stephen helped Ellen out of the litter and led her into the church. She was truly the fairest maiden Robin had ever seen. But now she was pale and drooping, and it was with a bent head and a sorrowful look that she went inside.

"Why do you not play, fellow?" the Bishop asked Robin.

"I will play in greater ways than your lordship thinks, but not until the right moment," Robin told him.

Now fair Ellen and Sir Stephen stood before the altar, and the Bishop himself prepared to read the wedding vows. Ellen looked around in bitter despair. Then Robin Hood strode forward in all his fluttering ribbons.

"Let me look upon the bride," he said in a loud voice. "Why, what have we here? Here be lilies in her cheeks, not roses such as befit a bonny bride. This is no fit wedding. I tell you, Sir Stephen, you may not make this lass your wife, for you are not her own true love."

At this, all stood amazed and knew not what to say. While everyone stared as if they'd been turned to stone, Robin lifted his horn to his lips and blew three blasts that echoed loud and clear. Little John and Will Stutely came up to stand on either side of Robin. "Here I am, good master, when you want me," called Friar Tuck from the organ loft.

Edward of Deirwold strode forward, raging, and would have seized his daughter, but Little John pushed him away. Then all the men-at-arms drew their swords, and it seemed that blood would wet the stones.

Suddenly, there was a bustle at the door. The men-at-arms fell back, and up the aisle came running eighteen men clad in Lincoln green, with Allan a Dale at their head.

Edward spoke in an angry voice. "Is it you, Allan, that has started all this mischief in a church?"

"No," said Robin, "that *I* have done. My name is Robin Hood. I mean you no harm," he added when the Bishop and the Prior shrank back in fear. "Here is fair Ellen's betrothed husband, and she shall marry him."

"No!" shouted Edward. "I am her father, and I say she will marry Sir Stephen."

"No, fellow," said Sir Stephen scornfully. "You may take your daughter back again. I did not know she loved another. Maiden, if you would choose a minstrel over a

high-born knight, then take your choice.'' He turned and, gathering his men about him, walked proudly up the aisle and out of the church.

Then the Bishop of Hereford said quickly, ''I, too, have no business here, so I will depart.'' But Robin Hood laid a hand on his arm.

''Stay, my Lord Bishop,'' he said. ''I have something to say to you.'' He turned to Edward of Deirwold. ''Give your blessing on your daughter's marriage. She will be married anyway, and it would be better for your blessing to be upon her.''

''If the girl wants to marry a minstrel, then let her,'' Edward said. ''I had thought to make a fine lady of her, but I will let her choose instead. She has my blessing.''

Then Friar Tuck came down from the loft and performed the marriage service. And so Allan and Ellen became man and wife.

At last, Robin turned to the Bishop of Hereford. "My Lord Bishop," he said, "remember that you promised me that if I played in such a way as to cause this fair lass to love her husband, you would give me whatever I asked. I have played my part, and she loves her husband. So now you must fulfill your promise. I think that golden chain about your neck would make a fair wedding present."

The Bishop's cheeks grew red with rage, but he had to do what Robin asked. Slowly he took the chain from around his neck. Robin flung it over Ellen's head so that it hung glittering on her shoulders, and thanked the Bishop heartily for his gift.

Robin Hood gathered his men together, and with Allan and his young bride in their midst, they all turned their footsteps toward the woodland. That night there was a feast held in the greenwood such as Nottinghamshire had never seen before.

A long time passed, and great changes came to England. King Henry died, and King Richard came to the crown. But none of these changes reached Sherwood's shaded lanes. Robin and his men dwelled as merrily as they ever had, with hunting and feasting and singing and woodland games brightening the course of their days.

One summer's day, Robin set out into the woods after breakfast. He strolled along a pleasant lane, thinking of nothing but the songs of the birds, until he came upon a man sitting beneath a broad-spreading oak tree. Never had Robin seen a figure like this one. From his head to his feet he was clad in a horse's hide. Even the hood on his head was made from the horse's skin! By his side lay a heavy broadsword and a stout yew bow.

"Hello, friend!" Robin called as he came up beside the odd figure. "Who are you? And what do you have upon your body? I have never seen such a sight before in all my life."

The other man pushed back the hood from his head and glared at Robin. His face was hard and cruel. "Who are you, rascal?" the stranger demanded in a rough voice.

"Speak not so sourly," Robin told him. "Have you fed upon vinegar and nettles this morning, that your speech is so stinging?"

"If you don't like my words," the stranger warned, "you'd best be going, for my deeds will match them."

"No, no, your speech is very pretty," Robin assured him. "But tell me, why do you wear such strange clothes?"

"I wear this coat to keep warm, fool," the stranger said, "and also because it protects me from sword thrusts. My name is Guy of Gisbourne, and I am an outlaw. I have come here because the Sheriff of Nottingham has promised me a pardon and one hundred pounds if I perform him a small service. He wishes me to hunt up a man named Robin Hood, and take him alive or dead. I care not if I slay this Robin Hood, for I would shed the blood of my own brother for one hundred pounds."

Robin listened to all of this and grew angry. He knew well of this Guy of Gisbourne, and of all the terrible deeds he had done. But he did not let his anger show as he said, "Truly, I have heard of you. I think there is no one in all the world that Robin Hood would rather meet than you."

Guy of Gisbourne gave a harsh laugh. "That would be an ill happening for Robin Hood. For the day he meets me, he shall die."

"But what if Robin Hood is the better man?"

"I bet my life that he is not!" Guy said firmly. "Some may call him a great archer, but I would not be afraid to stand against him."

"Well, many of us in Nottinghamshire are good with the long bow. Would you care to try a bout with me?"

Guy roared with laughter so that the woods rang with it. "You are a bold fellow to ask that. All right, I will try a bout with you."

Robin arose and cut a length of hazel from a thicket nearby. He stuck the thin shaft into the ground about eighty paces from where Guy of Gisbourne waited. "Let us see you split this wand, if you are indeed an archer," Robin said.

Guy made a face at the challenge, but he drew his bow. Twice he shot, but neither time did he hit the narrow shaft. "No man could hit such a mark as that!" he exclaimed.

Robin laughed. "Good fellow, if you are no better at the broadsword than you are with the bow and arrow, you will never overcome Robin Hood." Then he strung his bow and took his place.

Twice Robin shot. The first time, his arrow passed within an inch of the thin shaft. The second time, he split it fairly down the middle. Then he flung his bow upon the ground and drew his sword. "There, you bloody villain!" he cried fiercely. "Look your last upon the daylight, for this earth has been befouled by you long enough. I am Robin Hood!"

For a moment, Guy stared at Robin in wonder. Then his anger returned, and he grabbed his own sword. "I am glad to meet you!" he shouted, and the fight began.

Never did Sherwood see a fiercer fight, for each man knew that either he or the other must die. There would be no mercy. Up and down they fought, till all the green grass was crushed beneath their trampling feet. Soon the ground was sprinkled with bright red drops of blood.

At last, Guy of Gisbourne made a fierce and deadly thrust at Robin Hood. Robin leaped back, but caught his heel on a root and fell onto his back. As Guy stabbed at him, Robin caught the blade in his bare hand and turned the point away so that it plunged deep into the ground. Then he leaped up and ran his sword through Guy. The outlaw gave a wild cry, then fell to the ground and lay still.

Robin Hood wiped his sword and thrust it back into the scabbard. Standing over Guy of Gisbourne, he said to himself, "This is the first man I have killed since I shot the King's forester long ago. I often think bitterly of that first life I took. But of Guy of Gisbourne's murder, I am as glad as though I had slain a wild animal that was laying waste to a fair country."

A few months later, all Nottinghamshire was in a mighty stir. King Richard the Lionhearted was making a royal progress through England, and Nottingham Town was one of the stops on his travels.

It seemed to many of the good folk of Nottingham that the day of the King's arrival would never come. But at last it was time for the great event. The streets were alive with a restless sea of people, all gathered to catch a glimpse of their King.

At long last, the procession came into view. Eight and twenty heralds in velvet and cloth of gold rode forward. Each herald bore a silver trumpet in his hand. After them came a company of noble knights, holding lances tipped with colorful pennants that fluttered in the breeze. Behind the knights came all the noblemen of the country, wearing robes of silk, with golden chains and jewels hung all about them. Behind them were two riders, side by side. One was the Sheriff of Nottingham. The other bowed to the right and to the left as he rode. A mighty roar followed as he passed, for this was King Richard.

Among the crowd were Robin Hood and his merry band. When the Sheriff caught sight of them in their Lincoln green, he paled and nearly fell from his horse. But he did not mention the band of outlaws to the King, for he was ashamed that Robin Hood feared him so little that he dared to come within the very gates of Nottingham Town.

But that night, during the feast at the Guild Hall in Nottingham, King Richard said to the Sheriff, "I have heard much spoken about a certain fellow named Robin Hood and his band. Can you tell me about them?"

At these words, the Sheriff of Nottingham looked down gloomily and said, ''I can tell your majesty little, save that they are the boldest law-breakers in all the land.''

Then others at the table began to tell tales of Robin Hood and his merry adventures, until the King roared with laughter. ''I say, this is as bold and merry a knave as ever I heard of. I would like to meet him, and see something of his doings in Sherwood Forest. And perhaps I can do what you could not, Sheriff—clear the forest of Robin and his band.''

So the King and some of his men hatched a plan to meet Robin Hood. They would go into Sherwood disguised as friars, and allow Robin to take them to his hideaway. Everyone thought this was a good idea, except for the Sheriff. He refused to go.

The next morning, the King and his men dressed in their friars' robes, put hoods over their heads, and set out into the forest. They rode peacefully all morning. At last the King said, "I wish I had a better head for remembering things. Here we have started on our journey and brought nothing to drink with us. I would give fifty pounds for something to quench my thirst."

No sooner had the King spoken when out from the trees stepped a tall fellow with merry blue eyes. "Truly, brother," he said, "it would be inhumane not to answer your pleas. We keep a fine inn hereabouts, and for fifty pounds we will give you as noble a feast as you have ever tasted." He put his fingers to his lips and whistled, and threescore men in Lincoln green burst out of the trees.

"Who are you, you naughty rogue?" the King demanded. "Have you no respect for holy men such as we?"

"No," the fellow replied cheerfully. "I am Robin Hood. Now let me see your purse. I think anyone who would pay fifty pounds for a drink must be very wealthy indeed!

Show me your money, or I will have to take it from you by force.''

''Here is my purse,'' said the King sternly, ''but lay not your lawless hands about my person.''

''What proud words are these?'' mocked Robin. ''Are you the King of England that you would talk to me that way? Here Will, take this purse and see what is in it.''

Will Scarlet counted out fifty pounds and handed what was left back to the King. Then Robin and his men led their guests into the depths of the woodland, until they came to the open glade and the greenwood tree.

"Won't you take the hood from your face?" Robin asked the King.

"No, I will not," King Richard replied, for he was afraid he would be recognized if he did. Robin said no more about it.

When King Richard saw all the men gathered in the glade, he said to Robin, "You have a fine band of young men about you. I think King Richard himself would be glad of such a bodyguard."

"I tell you," Robin replied, "there is not one of us who would not pour out his blood like water for our King. We love him loyally for the sake of his brave deeds, and we would be honored to serve him."

Then the company drank to the King's health, never guessing that he was right in their midst. After that, there was a fine display of archery and other sports for the guests' amusement.

Suddenly, the sound of voices came through the trees. Little John, who had been out on his own adventures while Robin and the others entertained the King, burst into the glade. With him was Robin's good friend, Sir Richard of the Lea, an honorable and trustworthy nobleman.

"Make haste, dear friend!" Sir Richard shouted to Robin. "Gather your fellows and come with me! King Richard left Nottingham this morning, and he comes to hunt you in the woodlands. You must gather your men and stay at my castle until this danger is past." Then, seeing the band of friars gathered there, Sir Richard asked, "Who are these strangers?"

"Just some guests we met on the road this morning," Robin told him.

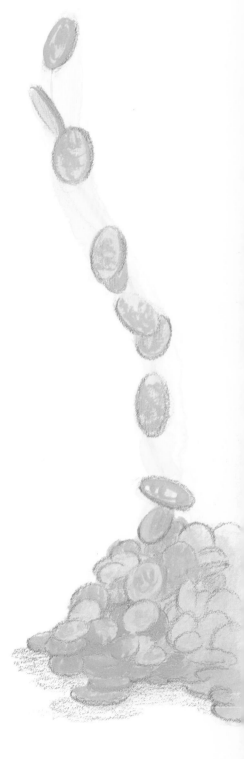

Sir Richard looked keenly at the tallest of the friars, and the King stared back at him. Suddenly, Sir Richard's cheeks grew pale, for he knew who it was that he looked upon. Quickly, he flung himself to his knees.

King Richard threw back his hood so that all could see his face. Everyone fell to their knees, so shocked they could not speak a word.

The King beckoned Robin to come to him. ''You are an outlaw,'' the King said to Robin, ''and you have broken my laws. But your loyalty has saved you from the harsh punishment you deserve. Still, I cannot let you roam the forest as you have done. Because you said you would be honored to serve me, I will take you back to London. Little John, Will Scarlet, and your minstrel, Allan a Dale, shall come with me also. As for the rest of your band, I shall make them royal foresters. I think it is wiser for them to be caretakers of Sherwood rather than outlaws.''

Then a great feast was spread on the grass, and all made merry. When they had finished, King Richard said he had never had such a tasty meal in all his life.

That night, the King slept in the forest on a bed of sweet green leaves. Early the next morning, he set forth for Nottingham Town, and Robin Hood and all his band went with him. The Sheriff did not know what to say when he saw Robin Hood in such high favor with the King, and his heart was filled with vexation.

The next day, the King took his leave of Nottingham Town. Robin Hood, Little John, Will Scarlet, and Allan a Dale said their goodbyes to the rest of the band, swearing they would come back to Sherwood often to see them. Then each mounted his horse and rode away in the train of the King, to share many new adventures in his service.